VOTE 4 AMELIA

by Marissa Moss
(and candidate Amelia)

Simon & Schuster Books for young Readers

New York   London   Toronto   Sydney
   ↑   ↑   ↑   ↑
Vote for me   here   and here   and here!

This notebook is dedicated to
Surya.
I nominate her for
Best Reader Ever!

SIMON & SCHUSTER BOOKS FOR YOUNG READERS
An imprint of Simon & Schuster Children's Publishing Division
1230 Avenue of the Americas, New York, New York 10020

SIMON & SCHUSTER BOOKS FOR YOUNG READERS
is a trademark of Simon & Schuster, Inc.

Amelia ® and the notebook design are
registered trademarks of Marissa Moss.   yay, Paula!
A Paula Wiseman Book ←   I vote 4 her!
Book design by Amelia
(with help from Lucy Ruth Cummins)

I won
by THIS
many votes!   The text for this book is hand-lettered.
                    Manufactured in China
              →   2 4 6 8 10 9 7 5 3 1

CIP data for this book is available
from the Library of Congress. ←   How about absentee ballots?

ISBN-13: 978-1-4169-2789-1
ISBN-10: 1-4169-2789-1

The school is covered with campaign slogans these days. Even bathroom stalls have posters taped on them, urging you to "Vote for Hudson for Prez" or "Vote for Olivia- I'll luv ya 4 it!" Some are pretty sloppy, some use cut-out letters so they look like ransom notes, and some are gorgeous works of art. Those are the ones I made — the beautiful ones.

When Carly decided to run for student body president, she wanted me to be her campaign manager— in other words, make her posters and think up catchy slogans. It's actually kind of fun. I like writing CARLY IS COOL! in big bubble letters. And I thought my dartboard idea was a work of genius. But there's a part that's not so good. Carly wanted me to run <u>with</u> her, so we could be on the Student Council together.

So while she's running for president, I'm running for secretary, and Leah is running for treasurer (the perfect job for her because she's so neat and organized).

The competition for president is fierce because a lot of people want the job, but really Carly only has to worry about one rival — Hudson.

Carly   vs.   Hudson
  ↓   ↓

↑

Carly is smart and popular. Kids like and respect her, and everyone knows how passionate she is about public causes after she collected all that money for hurricane victims last month.

↑

I don't know if Hudson is smart or not — it's hard to tell. But he's cute and VERY popular, one of the coolest kids in school, so he really doesn't have to be good at anything.

And me for secretary!
↓

I'm not cool, or popular, but I figure if Carly wins, I will too.

People will think of us together since we're best friends, and when they vote for her, they'll vote for me.

To be a good candidate, you have to be outgoing and energetic. You have to talk to people and make them like you. Those are things I'm _not_ good at. I'm better at behind-the-scenes kind of stuff — like dreaming up ideas for campaign slogans or posters and thinking of ways to make people pay attention to Carly.

Luckily, running for secretary is not exactly a high-profile job. It's not the sort of position people care passionately about. In fact, it's kind of like voting for chief dishwasher or head crosswalk guide. It's just a task _someone_ has to do. There's no glamour to it at all — none.

what does a secretary do anyway? I know they write down the minutes to each Student Council meeting, but is there anything else they do?

↓

I can take down minutes at least — I'm good at writing quickly. →

← Maybe not neatly, but quickly.

arrange things alphabetically?
↓

sharpen pencils?
↓

file folders?
↓
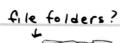

To be president, though, you need ideas — you need a reason people should vote for you, like plans for how you'd make things better at school. Some of the candidates have pretty silly ideas. Olivia promises that if she's elected, every Friday will be pizza day in the cafeteria instead of what it is now — Mystery Mush of Leftovers Day.

I like pizza, but that doesn't solve the leftover mush problem. The hairnet ladies will just make the mush on Thursday instead of Friday.

Carly takes the office of student body president more seriously than that. She has plans, BIG plans. Her number one priority is to take the TV sets in every classroom and put them to good use.

The way the school got the TVs in the first place was kind of sleazy.

Some company gave them to the school, but in return the principal had to agree to broadcast their "news" program once a week.

The problem is, it's not really news — it's more like propaganda with <u>lots</u> of ads to get kids to buy junk food, soda, clothes, shoes, all kinds of stuff no one needs. So we're forced to watch a bunch of ads with the illusion that there's some educational content to the programming.

Carly wants to change all that. She wants the kids in the Media class to use the donated audio-visual equipment to make our <u>own</u> news program, reporting on things that happen at school. I think that's a genius idea!

Of course, Carly wants to be one of the reporters. She'd be great at it!

And that's our story on the top prize winners in the science fair. Congratulations to all the students who worked so hard on their exhibits.

Now, to Luke with sports.

The things the other candidates are promising seem completely unrealistic next to Carly's plans. Eric says he'll make the schoolboard change the schedule so classes start at noon and kids can sleep late.

Of course, everyone loves that idea, but we all know that will never happen.

It makes for a fun campaign, though, even if it isn't realistic. To promote himself, Eric comes to school in pajamas, and his posters promise "No more baggy eyes!" and "feel rested and learn more!"

bed-head— he doesn't comb his hair →

He's giving away those sleep masks some people use on airplanes.

robe →

slippers →

↓

↑

It's so clever, people might vote for him just because he's packaged himself so well, even though no one believes he can really get the schedule changed.

Cassandra is running for president with the slogan "Vote for the Future." She says she'll get the school to provide everyone with a free laptop computer. All assignments would be submitted electronically, and all textbooks would be on the computers, so there'd be no more heavy backpacks.

If I thought she could really pull it off, even I would vote for her!

Who wouldn't trade a backbreaking load of books for a sleek, ultra-modern, light laptop?

this...   ...or this?

But we all know that will NEVER happen. Who will pay for computers? Who will put all the textbooks into a digital database? When you try to pin her down on those kinds of details, she doesn't have any answers.

The only candidate other than Carly with a realistic plan is Hudson, but it's not a reality I like.

His campaign slogan is "Vote for a Sweeter School — Vote Hudson!" He promises to have vending machines installed all over the school, so kids will never be far from a sugar fix. Since his dad is a Candy-Matic dealer, he can probably actually make this happen, but I don't think that's a good thing. I like candy as much as the next person, but I know it's not good for you.

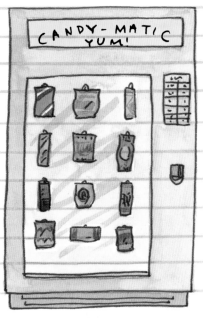

WARNING: Can cause cavities, sugar highs, and ← obesity! ↓

Hudson gives out candy bars to get kids to vote for him. Who can say no to free candy? I have to admit, I almost took one, but then I couldn't face Carly's disappointment, so I didn't.

↑
Carly especially HATES this idea! She doesn't eat junk food herself and makes her mom buy organic groceries, so to her this kind of thing is horrible pollution. Myself, I wouldn't mind one candy machine in the cafeteria, but NOT all over the school.

CAMPAIGN

IF U ♥ CHOCOLATE
VOTE 4 HALLIE
THE CHOCOLATE ♛QUEEN!

↑
She's not promising to give you chocolate, but simply the association of something delicious with her name is supposed to make you want to vote for her.

I WUV U DIS MUCH!

VOTE U-NICE!

the "Aw-how cute!" factor - who can resist those eyes?

who's against peace? Nobody! Does it matter that wars aren't topics for school decisions? Of course not! If you're against bad, mean war, you have to like Sandro, don't you? ↗

VOTE FOR WORLD PEACE!
VOTE FOR SANDRO!
PRESIDENT FOR PEACE!

SLOGANS

This is another unrealistic candidate. If it sounds too good to be true, it probably is. He'll still get some votes — I guarantee it!

NO MORE HOMEWORK!
VOTE 4 DAN!

TURN SCHOOL INTO **POOL**
OUT WITH DESKS!
IN WITH POOL TABLES!
VOTE 4 CARLOS!

↑ You know that Dan can't actually get rid of homework, but a voter can dream, can't they? It's wishful-thinking voting.

VOTE 4 HALLIE 4 A HALLIELICIOUS
S C H O O L !
HOORAY 4 HALLIE-DAYS!

↑ It means nothing, but it's certainly catchy, kind of like political popcorn — it's tasty, but it doesn't fill you up.

There was a meeting after school today for all the candidates. Ms. Oates, my art teacher, led it because she's the Student Council monitor, the one teacher who goes to all the Student Council meetings.

I call her Ms. Oates, even though she wants us to call her "Star." I've tried, but I just can't do it. ↓

She's not the kind of person you would think would do this kind of thing. Being in charge of rules isn't the way she teaches — she encourages freedom and creative expression, that kind of stuff.

I'm happy to see so many of you running for office. It's an important contribution you're making to our school.

Even if you personally don't win, the students do because you've given them a CHOICE, and CHOICE is what makes democracy work — choosing one set of ideas over another. That's what makes our country strong.

After congratulating us for running, she laid out the rules. Posters can only be a certain size. You can't put your poster over someone else's (and you can't take down your opponents' posters either). Then when the election is over, we're each responsible for cleaning up our own posters.

You're not supposed to "buy" votes, but giving out stuff is okay so long as you give it to EVERYBODY who asks, even people who say they're not voting for you. Handing out fliers is allowed, but littering them all over the place isn't.

There will be a debate where the candidates for president will each give a short statement and then answer students' questions. The rules are simple.

① No yelling.

② No name-calling.

③ No obscenities.

④ No speaking out of turn or interrupting.

If you break any ONE of those rules, Ms. Oates warned us, you'll be kicked out of the election. Then she made everyone shake hands with everyone else.

Hudson shook Carly's hand first.

I shook the hands of the other kids running for secretary. There are only two of them — like I said, it's not exactly a glamorous position.

Eunice is running for secretary with Eric — they're a team.

Vote double E's! Eunice and Eric!

This is very important work! It must be done neatly.

And it must be done well.

My slogan is "A good night's rest makes school best."

Bettina is running as an independent because she says she's a natural for the job.

That's me — tidy and careful ALL THE TIME!

No boys are running for secretary, which makes me especially suspicious of the job. Maybe it _is_ really like Chief Cafeteria Cook or Head Locker Room Janitor — a title no one wants (unless their friends pressure them to take it, like Carly did with me). I'm sure not neat and thorough, so maybe it would be best if Bettina won — better for her _and_ better for me.

Carly says I'm wrong. She thinks it'll be fun to be on the Student Council together. She thinks we can make real changes and improve our school. I'm just worried about improving my handwriting.

At least secretary is better than being Locker Room Janitor and having to dispose of rotting, smelly socks!

Running for treasurer is different. Either you think it's a really fun job because it involves money (and EVERYONE loves money!) or you want to be on the Student Council, and it's the easiest position you can think of. Or you're like Leah — a superorganized person who knows she's perfect for that kind of work.

STUDENT BODY OFFICES
I'D LIKE TO SEE

Since I'm not sure that presidents, secretaries, and treasurers really <u>do</u> anything, here are the positions I'd like students to have:

↓

Chief Art Supply Buyer

Director of Elective Choices

No more markers-and-construction-paper projects — it's time to make a mosaic!

I LOVE the class on the Art of the Comic!

Yeah, I'm taking that next semester. Right now I'm in Joke-Telling — it's hilarious!

And now change classes to the latest from your favorite group...

Scratch off the trip to the chicken-packing factory — the beach sounds MUCH more educational!

P.A. System D.J.

Director of Field Trips

After the meeting Carly and Leah came over to my house so we could talk about our campaign strategy.

The thing to focus on now is the debate. I've got to be prepared — I have to sound like a strong, smart leader, someone with ideas.

↑
I don't know why Carly's worried. She always sounds smart and strong.

I don't think the debate is a problem. You're a way better speaker than anyone else. The problem is, Hudson's <u>so</u> popular AND he's giving away candy. Those are reasons enough to vote for him.

↑
I agree with Leah. Hudson is tough competition, especially if the election turns into a popularity contest, like most student elections do.

Leah's right. What can <u>we</u> give out that's better than candy but doesn't cost a lot? And it has to be something that reminds kids of Carly.

Even pooling all our allowances, we don't have a big campaign budget. Leah said we should look at what we <u>are</u> rich in — creativity, talent, and artistic skill (since both Leah and me are good at drawing). Those sound like good assets, but how do they translate into an attention-getting giveaway?

We needed a break, so we went into the kitchen for a snack. Unfortunately Cleo was there, chomping on one of her strange sandwich creations. (The worst one was peanut butter, pickle, and avocado – GROSS!) The sight of her made me lose my appetite.

she wasn't exactly cheering everyone else up either.

Hey, Carly, I see you're running against Hudson. He's tough to beat. The only thing kids love more than candy is TV, and you're Miss Anti-TV.

"I'm not anti-TV," Carly said. "I'm against the school force-feeding us ads. I want the TV to be OUR TV."

"That's it!" I yelled. "That's our slogan AND our give-away!"

Everyone looked at me like I was making no sense.

"Here, I'll show you," I explained. I ran back to my room and made a quick model.

It was a small card shaped like a TV set.

CHANGE THE CHANNEL
TAKE OVER COMMERCIAL TV!

You pulled away the card inserted into the TV to see the picture under it.

The picture beneath showed the school mascot, Rocky Raccoon, and the rest of the slogan.

"See!" I said, demonstrating how the cards worked. "It's a positive message — not anti-TV, but PRO student TV. And it's an active thing. You change the channel by changing the picture."

Even Cleo was impressed. "Not bad," she nodded. "But it'll be a <u>lot</u> of work to make enough of these to hand out to everybody."

Even with the three of us, it was slow going — and BOOOOOOOORING!

The only way to keep ourselves from falling asleep was to spice things up with several different versions of the card.

one with Carly

one with lots of kids

one with aliens

Then we started getting really silly. In order to make so many cards, we had to make it fun for ourselves.

In a few days we had finally made enough of the TV cards that we could start giving them out. They turned out to be so cute, everybody wanted one — even the teachers.

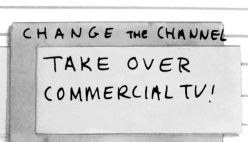

CHANGE the CHANNEL

TAKE OVER COMMERCIAL TV!

the finished card — they were actually fun to make. in _small_ batches!

Even Hudson liked them. He came up to us at lunch and asked for one.

"Where are those clever cards everyone's talking about?" He winked at Carly. "Don't I get one?"

"Sure," she said, handing him one. "_You_ can vote for me too, you know."

He played with the card and smiled. "Who knows? Maybe I will." He winked again and left.

"Can you believe that?" Leah was outraged. "He's FLIRTING with you! Does he think you'll fall in love with him and drop out of the race? The nerve of him!"

"Look!" I said. "Everyone _else_ seems to be in love with him." A group of girls surrounded him, twittering and giggling. "If he wins, that's why."

Carly shrugged. "He can't help it if girls like him, and there's nothing _I_ can do about it either. I've just got to be as strong a candidate as I can. He can flirt all he wants — he can even ask me out. I'm still running for president."

Leah looked stunned. "You'd go out with him?"

Carly smiled. "Maybe. He _is_ cute. But so what? That doesn't change the election."

Leah didn't say anything after that, but she didn't look happy. I didn't know what to think, so I just finished my lunch, trying not to hear the girls oohing and aahing over something Hudson said. Carly's too smart to turn into one of _them_, I told myself.

Suddenly I was glad Carly had asked me to run for secretary. What if she'd asked Hudson? Or some other boy?

I wanted to be on her team and help her win. I didn't care about being on the student council — I cared about being Carly's best friend.

As the election gets closer, the campaign posters seem to be multiplying — THEY'RE EVERYWHERE! It's hard to find a space that's not taken. I'm trying to be creative, not only in what the posters say, but in where I put them.

on the basketball backboard ↓

SCORE A POINT FOR CARLY—
VOTE SMART!

above the only drinking fountain that works in the 300 wing ↓

FOR A REFRESHING CHANGE —
CHANGE THE CHANNEL
CARLY 4 PRESIDENT!

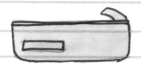

MAKE A CHANGE THAT MATTERS!
CHANGE THE CHANNEL
WITH CARLY FOR
PRESIDENT!

↑ by the recycling bins in the cafeteria

GET THE NEWS THAT MATTERS 2 U!
CARLY 4 PREZ!

↑ near the library door

MEDIA CENTER

EE

VOTE DOUBLE
E'S!
ERIC AND EUNICE

Bettina
a good bet
4 secretary

HUDSON
WE LUV U,
HUDSON!

Jehisse
will make
your
$ $ $
COUNT!

$
$
$
$
$
$
$
$

Carly says I'm doing a
great job. She hasn't said anything
more about Hudson, but I noticed
that when he offered her a candy
bar, she didn't take it. That's a
good sign — she's still more
interested in the election than in
him. It'd better stay that way!
　　There's still work to do to get
ready for the debate. Leah and I
don't have to make a speech,
but we're helping Carly with
hers, and we've set up a practice
debate after school with Leah
being Hudson.

Olivia
4 PREZ!
THE PIZZA
WINS!

VOTE
4
HOWARD!
Y NOT?

He's a star!
HUDSON
4 PRESIDENT
!!!

FOR A GOOD NITE'S SLEEP

ERIC 4
PRESIDENT!

VOTE
4
MEL

LEAH FOR
$ $
TREASURER

And we're still handing out the TV cards. Hudson keeps sending his friends over to take them, but I know what he's doing — he's making us waste our precious resources on his loyal henchman, people who will never vote for Carly. And there's nothing I can do about it. The campaign rules say giveaways must be for everyone. Otherwise, it's buying votes.

I just clench my teeth and try to get it over with as quickly as possible.

Here! Take it and go away!

That gave me the idea to do the same thing back to them. Now my backpack is FULL of candy bars. I got one by the gym, another in the library, another from some Hudsonite by my locker. Everywhere I go, there's another "Vote for Hudson" campaign worker. How did he get so many people to work for him? Wait a minute, it's obvious — he's PAYING them with candy (something he seems to have an infinite supply of, thanks to his dad).

"Well, there should be!" I was disgusted.

Ms. Oates pursed her lips (something I'd never seen her do before - she's not the pursing lips type).

"We have to work with the rules that are already in place," she said. "If you want to change them for the next election, you'll have to be elected to the Student Council in this one."

I was so exasperated, I wanted to scream. Now I know why kids call her "Astronaut Oates" (instead of "Star" like she wants). She's too far out in space to see how unfair it all is. I guess I should pay more attention to teachers' nicknames. They aren't just arbitrary — there's some truth in them, maybe a lot.

Mr. Lambaste was my mean English and Social Studies teacher last year. Now I have him for Study Hall, which isn't as bad. He's called Mr. L. or Smelly-L or Smell-O because no one likes him — that's reason enough.

Mrs. Church, my math teacher last year, is called "Big Bird." That comes from being called "Mrs. Chirp" first because she's always so cheery. Also she's tall and lanky and when she's excited about some brilliant math equation, she flaps her arms like wings.

Oooh, now wait till we try this with fractions!

Ms. Reilly, my old science teacher, has the nickname "The Professor" because she never stops lecturing. She's a good teacher, but she's always trying to cram more information into you than your brain can hold.

This little factoid about spores and ferns is simply fascinating...

Mr. Hamlin, the other 6th-grade science teacher, is called "Homework Hamlin" because he assigns massive amounts of homework.

I've never seen a worksheet I didn't like. This one is due tomorrow.

Mr. Castillo, the French teacher (the other one, not the one I have), is called "Mr. Caster Oily" because being in his class is like swallowing some nasty medicine. →

I hear talking in English! Jamais! En français!!

Ms. Singh has the nickname "Elvis" because she loves Elvis Presley and plays his songs whenever she gets a chance. Sometimes she → even sings along. Leah has her for math and thinks she's the best.

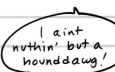

I aint nuthin' but a hound dawg!

Mr. Klein, the P.E. teacher, is called "The Devil." No explanation is necessary. →

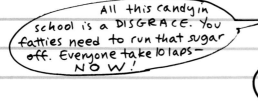

All this candy in school is a DISGRACE. You fatties need to run that sugar off. Everyone take 10 laps— NOW!

Then we'll get serious about calisthenics — and I mean SERIOUS!

I thought maybe I could give Hudson a nickname that would show people who he really is, so they don't just judge him on looks or coolness. But the only nickname that would stick is "Hunk" and I DON'T want him called that. "Weasel" is more like it, but I'm probably the only person who'd use it — except for Leah. She REALLY doesn't trust him.

I heard that Hudson is going to ask Carly to the dance next week. That is so GROSS!

So what if he asks her? She won't say yes.

How do you know?

?

Actually, I didn't know. I hoped, I wanted her to say no. Maybe I could convince her to turn him down. If she was going to say yes in the first place, which I didn't think she'd do.

On the way home from school, I decided to ask Carly about it directly. I was going to say something smooth and persuasive, but I ended up blurting out, "You wouldn't go to the dance with Hudson, would you?"

Carly looked at me, surprised. "Why would he ask me? Isn't he Luanne's boyfriend?"

"They broke up," I said, "and rumor has it he's going to ask you."

Carly smiled. "Well, maybe I _would_ go with him."

"You can't!" I yelled.

She shrugged. "Just because we're competing for the same thing doesn't mean we can't be friends."

"But he's only trying to trick you, to get you to trust him, and then..."

"Then what?" Carly pressed.

I wasn't sure what, but something bad, I knew that. I shook my head. "He's up to something, I'm sure of it." I didn't want to fight with Carly, but the conversation wasn't going at all the way I'd hoped.

Carly stopped walking and cocked her head. "Did you hear that?" she asked.

"Hear what?" Suddenly I was afraid Hudson was spying on us. "I don't hear anything."

"That whimpering noise. It's coming from over there." Carly pointed to some trash.

smelly, rotting vegetables ↓

a good place for a spying rat to hide ⟶

I walked over to the garbage, sure I'd find some kind of rat — human or animal. But it wasn't anything like that.

It was a puppy, a cute, adorable puppy with big, brown eyes. →

It was whimpering and shivering, poor thing. ←

"Oh, poor baby!" Carly soothed, picking it up. "Look at you — no collar, no owner. Are you lost? Who would leave such a cutie by the trash?"

The puppy wagged its tail and licked Carly's nose for an answer. ↓

"I wish I could take her home," I said (I could see it was a girl). "But my mom has a strict no-pets rule — not even goldfish."

"Maybe I can keep her," Carly said. "I've been begging my parents for a dog forever. They always say no because of my dad's allergies, but I bet if they saw this cutie-pie, they couldn't turn her away. I mean, who could?"

I took the puppy from her, stroking its soft fuzz. I didn't even mind her nipping at my hands — the teeth were so tiny, they were like little pin pricks. I hugged her, and she licked my ear. It tickled so much, I couldn't help laughing.

"You're right. Who could resist such a little furball?" I sighed, and handed her back to Carly. "Only one person — my mom."

"Yeah," Carly agreed. "Your mom is the most unsentimental person I've ever met. I mean, not even a goldfish — that's cold."

I shrugged. "She doesn't like messes."

Carly rolled her eyes. "Like fish are so messy? Yeah, they're always tracking in dirt and clawing at the furniture."

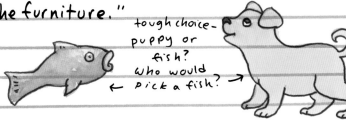

tough choice—
puppy or fish?
who would
← pick a fish? →

We were planning on going to my house, but now that we had the puppy, we decided to go to Carly's. On the way there we thought of all the reasons we could give for why Carly should get to keep the dog.

By the time we got there, we had a pretty good list.

Yes, Puppy!

No, Puppy

The puppy needed a good home.

Carly's dad is allergic.

Carly would learn to be SUPER-responsible, since she would do ALL the work.

← All these reasons way outbalance the one lame reaso. not to keep the dog. plus Carly's brother would love the puppy. they've been begging for years to get one. It was a solid case!

Carly would vacuum every day to control any dog hair so her dad wouldn't have allergies and her mom would have a clean house.

At least we thought it was a good list, a clear slam dunk for the puppy. Unfortunately Carly's mom didn't like our list as much as we did.

Now, baby, I know you want a dog and this one is sure cute, no doubt about that!

But you have no idea how much work a dog can be. You have to feed it, walk it, train it, take care of it when it gets sick, clean up its messes.

You have <u>no</u> idea! But the reason I'm saying no isn't about all that. You know why I have to say no and why you shouldn't have even asked in the first place.

I do NOT know that! And how could I NOT ask? Look at this poor thing! She needs a home and you're turning her away coldheartedly. It's not like I went out and got a puppy — this puppy found me!

Ms. Tremain looked sad, but that didn't mean she was going to change her mind.

"Listen, Carly, I know you've already fallen in love with this dog." She reached over and stroked the puppy's head. "But your dad's health comes first. No dogs, not even superadorable ones like this cutie."

"But..." Carly tried again.

"No buts," her mom said firmly. "This isn't about whether you're responsible enough. I <u>know</u> how responsible you are — and believe me, if your dad weren't allergic, I'd say yes in a heartbeat. But he is, and I've seen him when he gets too close to dogs." She shuddered and frowned. "It's <u>not</u> a pretty sight — rashes, swelling, sneezing. Uh, uh!"

"Then what about this poor, innocent puppy?" Carly wailed. "Amelia can't take her - you know her mom!"

And then Ms. Tremain said the dreaded words: "There's alway the animal shelter."

we were both stunned. We ← knew what → <u>that</u> meant.

"Now, don't look at me like that," Ms. Tremain went on. "The animal shelter will find a good home for this baby. That's what they <u>do</u>. That's where people go when they're looking to adopt a puppy."

"But," Carly gulped, "if no one picks her, they'll put her to sleep. Isn't that also what they do?"

"Only as a very last resort. It doesn't happen often, and I'm <u>sure</u> someone will give this dog a home." Carly's mom tried to reassure us. I wanted to believe her, but what if it was a bad season for puppies, like there were too many of them or people were too busy to get new pets?

what if there was already a long line of adorable puppies waiting for a home? How could we be sure our puppy would be picked?

Carly and I looked at each other. We were both thinking the same thing. It wasn't good.

The puppy didn't know what to think.

Carly's mom sighed and shook her head. "Look at you two! You'd think I was condemning that poor puppy to death!" She sighed again, loudly. "Oh, all right," she said. "Here's the deal — I'm so sure that somebody will give this baby a home that if she's not adopted by the end of 3 weeks, we'll take her <u>until</u> — and I emphasize ONLY UNTIL — we can find a family for her ourselves. How's that?"

Carly grinned and ran to hug her mom. "Thanks, Mama, I knew you couldn't be cruel to an innocent, sweet puppy."

"Yeah, thanks, Ms. Tremain," I echoed. "We can find someone to take the puppy if we just have some time."

For now, though, we had to keep our part of the deal and take the puppy to the animal shelter. It wasn't far, so Carly and I decided to walk. We tied a rope around the puppy's neck. It felt like she was really ours, at least until we got to the animal shelter.

The puppy wasn't used to a leash and she was so excited, she zigzagged all over the place. When we got tired of untangling the rope, we picked her up and carried her.

We were almost there when we saw Hudson across the street. I would've kept on walking, but he yelled, "Hey!" at Carly (not at me) and smiled. So she stopped and waited for him to catch up to us.

"Hey, yourself," she said. I didn't say anything.

"Cute girl with cute puppy. Where are you going?" He wasn't looking at the dog — he was looking at Carly. Then he leaned down and stroked the puppy's soft head.

"Bite him!" I sent her a mental message. "Bite him HARD!" But my mental telepathy is a bit weak, and the puppy just wagged her whole body and licked Hudson's fingers.

I couldn't believe it — Carly started telling Hudson the whole story, like he was a <u>friend</u>.

...so we're taking her to the shelter and if no one adopts her, we'll come back and keep her until we can find her a home.

I might be able to save you the trouble. I'd love to take her! My parents already said I could have a dog — they're just waiting for some breeder to call. I'll tell them I want <u>this</u> dog.

"Really?" Carly asked. "You'll give her a home?"

"Don't be so surprised!" Hudson laughed. "Who could resist her?" He picked up the puppy and let her lick his ear. "I think I'll name her Munchkin."

I wanted to gag. I mean, I was glad he was taking the puppy. Even if he was a creep, he was better than the animal shelter. But he was so oily-fake, he made my skin crawl. Couldn't Carly see it?

I guess she couldn't because she handed him the rope leash and said, "Thanks, Hudson. You're pretty great."

"I'm the one who should thank you." He smiled that sugary grin again. "Thanks for the puppy - and for the cool story about how you rescued her."

I should have known there was something suspicious about him saying that, but I just wanted to get away.

"We have to get going," I interrupted. "Bye."

"Bye, Carly." Hudson scooped up the puppy and walked off. He looked so pleased with himself, you'd think he'd gotten away with something.

Wasn't that nice of him? We don't have to worry about the puppy.

No, now we have to worry about YOU — what's got into you? He's a total creep, can't you tell?

"Come on, Amelia," Carly said. "You just can't believe anything good about Hudson. Stop being so suspicious."

"That's not true!" I disagreed. "It was nice of him to take the puppy — really, that's great. Maybe he'll be a good master, but there's something about him I don't trust."

"That's only because he's my main competition."

Maybe that was it. I hoped for Munchkin's sake he <u>was</u> a nice person.

HE KNOWS HIS STUFF!
UNDERSTANDS STUDENTS!
DOES HIS BEST!
SUPER GUY!
ON TOP OF THINGS!
NAME HIM PRESIDENT!!

V
O
T
E

CHANGE THE CHANNEL
CARLY!
VOTE FOR STUDENT CONTROL OVER TV!

You see these posters ALL OVER school.

We have to squeeze in Carly's posters. →

We needed to forget about Hudson the person and Hudson the puppy rescuer. It was time to focus on Hudson the candidate.

The debate is coming up, and Carly needs to do way better than Hudson in it. I know she's been practicing a lot. Leah and I have heard her statement so many times, we could almost give it for her.

Carly's a pro. No matter how much she likes Hudson (and she's still not admitting anything), she's not going to go easy on him in the debate. She's an expert arguer, no matter how sugary or sleazy Hudson might get.

So I'm not worrying about that. I have something else on my mind. Our campaign posters keep disappearing. Every time I put up a new "Vote to Change the Channel! Vote for Carly" banner, by the next day it's gone. You would think someone would have seen who's taking down the posters, but no one knows — or no one's telling. Naturally, I have my suspicions.

POSSIBLE POSTER PILFERERS

The first choice would be someone campaigning for the same office. That means all the other presidential candidates.

↑

Hudson — why would he bother? He's so popular, does he need to cheat? He shouldn't, but he's the one I trust the least.

↑

Olivia — she doesn't seem mean enough. Besides, I get the feeling she doesn't care enough about winning to bother.

↑

Eric — I guess it could be him, but I actually like Eric, so I hope not. He has a good sense of humor and isn't the sleazy type.

↑

Cassandra — she definitely cares a LOT about winning, but if it's her, why doesn't she take down other posters, not just Carly's?

↑

Sandro — I still haven't figured out why he's even running. His slogan is "Make my day - Vote for Sandro." I want to know why I should care?

↑

Hallie — she thinks it's a beauty contest, not a political election. And the way some guys look at her, she may be right.

Or the poster thief could be an enemy of Carly, someone who doesn't like her. That's a pretty short list.

↑
Maxine — she's been mad at Carly ever since she dumped her as a friend— I mean, Maxine dumped Carly, not the other way around. She thought Carly would be devastated and pine away for her. And maybe Carly would have, but she figured out what a manipulative creep Maxine is and let her know it!

↑
Graham — he's been nasty to Carly because he asked her to a dance and she said no. She didn't mean to hurt his feelings and she turned him down as nicely as she could, but he still hasn't forgiven her. Now he says she's a stuck-up snob and he wouldn't go out with her if she begged him. Really?

After Hudson, who's suspect #1, I think it's probably someone from the second group, even though there are fewer suspects. Maxine seems the most likely to me. Leah is sure it's Hudson. Carly says she has no idea and doesn't really care (except she's sure it's NOT Hudson).

She thinks we should focus on putting up new posters and not worry about what happened to the old ones. That's easy for her to say — it's a _lot_ of work to make new posters and find some space to put them. And then the next day I have to do the same thing all over again. The posters are getting pretty sloppy.

The first batch looked good. ↓

The second batch was okay. ↓

The third batch looked kind of desperate. ↓

CHANGE THE CHANNEL!

VOTE FOR CARLY
TV BY THE STUDENTS, FOR THE STUDENTS, AND OF THE STUDENTS.

VOTE 4 CHANGE
VOTE 4 STUDENT POWER
VOTE 4 CARLY
4 PREZ!

I SAID: **VOTE 4 CARLY!** DO IT!

I thought I might get an idea of who was taking down the posters if some other candidate's always took their place, but that's no indication. Once a new poster for Eric went up where one of Carly's was. Another time, it was a poster for Jenisse, who's not even running for president — she wants to be treasurer. Sometimes the space is even left blank. There's no suspicious pattern to it.

I tried to trick Maxine into admitting that she was the culprit.

I see you've graduated from sending nasty notes to removing good ones.

What **are** you talking about?

A campaign poster is like a note – a note to everyone. Taking one down is like taking down a note, get it?

What A RE you talking about?

She acted like she didn't understand what I was saying. Maybe I should have been more direct.

Leah tried a different tactic. She followed Hudson around all day, but she didn't have any more success than I did.

Just because I didn't catch him red-handed, doesn't mean he's not responsible. He probably has friends – or candy-workers – doing his dirty deeds for him.

Carly said it's time to stop worrying about the posters. We have a debate to win — tomorrow!

The key to public speaking is to talk loudly, clearly, and slowly.

And to be passionate about your point of view— no dull monotone, no boring mumbling, no droning on and on.

I'm glad it's not me going up there in front of the whole school. Carly will do a great job. She's not nervous at all.

How to Give a Great Speech

Ten Easy Tips to Terrific Public Speaking

I did it my waaaaaaaay!

1. Pretend you aren't giving a speech, but doing spoken karaoke— ham it up and have fun!

2. Practice your speech so much, you could give it in your sleep.

Fourscore and seven years ago... SNOOOORE...

3. Turn your speech into a rap song. It'll be easier to remember that way.

Snap!

I just need to get my beat going and then I can start.

4. Mime your speech or act it out like in charades — that way you don't have to worry about speaking loudly and clearly.

...sounds like wall?

Ball? Fall? Tall?

Ashk nob wadu cardu foya cutrg ...

5. Practice your speech with a giant jawbreaker in your mouth. If you can be understood with that in your cheek, you'll be superclear without it.

6. Use audiovisual props — that way you'll have your audience's attention even if you don't speak well.

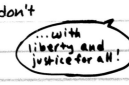

7. Turn your speech into a jump-rope rhyme. You'll be so busy jumping, you'll forget to be nervous.

8. Make your speech short and exciting — that way no one will get bored and you'll have less time to make a mistake.

9. Use a phone as a prop. Don't actually make a call — just holding it to your ear while you talk will make you much more relaxed.

10. Forget about the speech and just offer to answer questions instead.

THE GREAT

Carly doesn't need any of those tips. She's a natural speaker. ↓

Eric was in his pajamas and bathrobe just like I suggested in tip #6. ↙

↑

I was more nervous watching her than she was standing in front of the whole school! She was great, like I knew she would be, and kids clapped the loudest for her.

↑

Eric was okay, except he tried to make his point about how tired starting school at 8:00 am. makes him by falling asleep in the middle of his speech!

↑

Hallie chose the short and sweet method - "Hello." (BIG smile.) "Vote for me. Bye!"

↑

Sandro turned his speech into a cheerleading cheer. It woke everyone up after Eric and Hallie.

DEBATE

Ms. Oates was the moderator, of course. →

↑
She introduced everyone, made sure no one talked too long (NOT a problem), then asked questions for the debate part.

↑
Cassandra was <u>so</u> technical, it was hard to focus on what she was saying — "wireless Internet... speed of transmission... amount of data..." It was more of a lecture than a speech.

↑
I have to admit Hudson was okay. He didn't say anything fascinating, but he was loud, clear, and concise. He talked more about candy than student government, and some kids thought that was a GOOD thing.

↑
Olivia started by reading a recipe for pizza. It sounds like a catchy idea, but if you've ever read a recipe out loud, you know how boring that can be. It's like reading the phone book!

Ms. Oates asked questions like "Why should you represent all the other students to the school administration? What can you do for them that no one else can?" I wouldn't have known what to say — and some of the candidates had that same problem. Olivia, for example, said, "I would speak out for pizza lovers everywhere!" Sounds okay, but what does it _mean_? Eric said he would sleep through Student Council meetings, so the principal would get the hint that school starts too early. And that's supposed to make us want to vote for him?

Hudson acted like he was giving students exactly what they wanted when he promised that he — and only he — could deliver a candy-snack machine to every hallway. I wonder if that's _really_ what kids want and need. I'm all for the occasional snack, but in _every_ hallway? We'll have the fattest school ever!

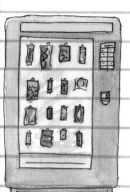

← But Hudson made a convincing sales pitch. He had something to offer that nobody else could give.

The way everyone applauded, you would think he was promising each kid their own home-theater system, not a fast-track to no more money and a lot more tummy.

I wish he'd brought some visual aids — a graphic before-and-after picture would have been better than any argument he could make.

Carly, of course, answered all the questions better than anyone. She was smart and funny and had great ideas. She was SO much better than the others, the election seemed like a slam dunk — even if we lost all of our posters.

A whole mob of kids came up to say how well Carly did and that they would definitely vote for her. She made a BIG impression. But Hudson had a circle of kids around him, too — not as many as Carly (that made me smile), but more than anyone else except her.

"I think you've got Hudson beat," I said.

Carly grinned. "And you were worried I'd go easy on him — as if I'd lose on purpose! I want to win, no matter how cute my main opponent is."

Leah clapped Carly on the back. "You want to win this thing because you want to make a difference. The other kids are running for office to have fun or to test how popular they are. You're the only one with a serious plan."

"I don't know about that," Carly said. "Hudson's serious about his plan too."

"Candy machines everywhere? That's a plan?" Leah frowned. "That's just about making money — for his dad. He's the one with the vending machine company. I bet Hudson gets a cut."

"Yeah," I agreed. "Who really benefits from the machines? Hudson's dad will make a fortune!" It all seemed sleazy to me.

Just then Maya walked up, munching on a candy bar.

"Carly, you were terrific!" she said. "I'm voting for you, but after you win, could you work with Hudson to get at least a couple of those candy machines? Have you tried the Mellow Bars? They're delicious!"

"If I win, getting vending machines isn't high on my list of priorities. I have to be honest with you — if you really want candy, you should vote for Hudson."

Maya looked hurt. "I think you'd be a better president."

Carly sighed. "I guess I'm worried a lot of kids will think that but will still vote for Hudson because they like chocolate. I can't keep his promises."

"If they do that, then they're stupid voters and they'll get what they deserve," I said.

"Yeah? What about the rest of us?" Leah demanded. "I don't even like candy! So you're saying I'll be stuck with Hudson because other kids can't control their appetites?"

"I'm not saying anything like that." Carly took the candy wrapper from Maya, wadded it up, and pitched it into the trash can. "I'm just saying I hope people will vote for who will make the best president, not who will fill their stomach with sugar. And if you vote for me," she looked at Maya, "it should be because you support me, not because you want me to follow some other guy's plan, especially when it's one I don't agree with."

"You're right, Carly, I'm sorry." Maya did look sorry. "I just have a soft spot for Mellow Bars."

Carly and I looked at each other. We were both worried that a lot of kids were like Maya. That meant no matter how great Carly was in her speech or the debate, she wouldn't win. Kids would choose chocolate over anything else.

Carly might have been worried about Hudson getting votes for candy, but Hudson was worried too. He knew that Carly had done better in the debate than he had. He hadn't seemed smart or capable or funny — Eric came off better than him in those areas. Hudson acted like a candy salesman, not a president.

I could tell he was worried because he started giving out lots more chocolate — so much candy that the principal decided the giveaways were getting out of control and he banned any more handouts.

That made Hudson even more nervous. Without the temptation of sugar, how would he get enough votes? At lunch I heard him arguing with his friends, yelling that they weren't any help now that they weren't giving out chocolate. And he isn't flirting with Carly anymore either. He doesn't even look at her when he passes by.

Candy wrappers were everywhere, and kids were manic on sugar highs. The teachers hated it!

It's only a week until the election, and Hudson must be feeling desperate because he did something really ugly, something I never would have thought him capable of, even at his sleaziest.

He started a smear campaign against Carly. And he used the puppy to do it.

Leah was the first to notice something was wrong. "What's going on, Carly?" she asked. "People are looking at you funny. There's some kind of rumor spreading about you — and it's NOT a good one. Do you know what kids are saying?"

She didn't. I didn't. We hadn't heard a thing. As we walked to the library, Carly turned to notice every kid we passed. When she smiled and waved at people she knew, no one smiled back. They wouldn't look her in the face

"You're right!" Carly wailed. "It's something really horrible — no one will even glance at me. What _is_ it?"

"Come on, think!" I said. "Did ANYTHING happen that could have made someone mad at you? Did you have a fight with anyone? Is Maxine up to her old tricks, writing nasty notes _about_ you instead of _to_ you?"

Carly shook her head. She looked really upset, like she would cry any minute.

As soon as we came into the library, everyone turned to stare at us — and not in a good way — then they started whispering to each other. It felt like we'd walked in without any clothes on.

It was like one of those nightmares where you're at school and you realize you forgot to get dressed — only this wasn't a bad dream, it was real!

↓

First I felt terrible, but then I got mad. We hadn't done ANYTHING to deserve that kind of treatment, and I was going to find out what was behind it all.

I marched up to the closest knot of kids.

"Hey!" I hissed. "What's going on? Why is everyone looking at us like that?"

"It's not you," a girl answered. "It's Carly. She seemed so cool, but to practically murder a puppy..."

"What _are_ you talking about?" I squawked.

"You don't know?" Her eyebrows shot up and almost flew off her forehead. She was excited to find someone who didn't know such juicy gossip and she couldn't wait to tell me.

It was ugly — very ugly. And it was Hudson who started it all.

He needed a weapon to use against Carly, and he chose the cutest, softest, sweetest thing he could find.
→

MUNCHKIN!
←

According to this girl, Hudson had the puppy with him after school yesterday. Naturally puppies are people magnets and everyone came up to pet her and ooh over how adorable she was. (He'd tied a bandanna around her neck, so she was especially cute.)

Then, as kids played with Munchkin, he told them how he found her when Carly was taking her to the animal shelter. Hudson claimed Carly was going to abandon Munchkin to an awful fate when he stepped in and rescued her. He insisted he would give the puppy a good home since Carly was so cruelly throwing her away.

"He saved that puppy's life," the girl finished. "I had no idea Carly was that cold."

"She's not!" I snapped. "The whole thing is a lie from start to finish. I was there — I know!"

Suddenly everyone was staring at me, waiting for my explanation.

I was ready to scream at all of them that Hudson was a manipulative creep!

Except I had the sinking feeling that no one would believe me. After all, we _were_ taking Munchkin to the shelter, and Hudson _did_ adopt her and give her a home. The other details — that Carly would have come back for the puppy if no one took her — sounded suspiciously like a lame lie.

"Well?" the girl asked. "What really happened?"

"Hudson twisted the facts — Carly was never going to abandon the puppy." I knew I sounded desperate even as I said it.

"Uh-huh," the girl nodded, looking like she didn't believe a word. "Right. Sure." Her friends smiled and nodded too. "But she _was_ taking the puppy to the animal shelter?" she pressed.

"Yes, but..." I bit my lip. I was afraid I was confirming the ugly rumor rather than refuting it. "Her mom said she had to wait a couple of weeks, but if no one took the puppy home, then Carly could come back and get her."

"So Hudson told the truth?" It was like she didn't even hear my explanation.

I always thought of the → truth as a single thing, whole and simple.

← Now I saw how it could be chopped up, crumbled, turned upside-down and not be the truth at all.

"No!" I yelled. "I mean, yes, kind of, a sliver of the truth, a crumb, but NOT the whole thing." I gave up. I went back to Carly and Leah and explained what had happened.

"He's using Munchkin against you," I summed it up. "And who can resist those big, brown puppy-dog eyes?"

"That makes me sick!" said Leah. "It's like false advertising — he's telling enough of the truth to be trustworthy, but leaving out the most important parts so people will get the wrong impression. It's a total distortion!"

Carly was crushed.

It's like saying, "Eat candy — it will give you energy" without mentioning it will also make you fat.

What do I do now? This is about more than the election — it's about my reputation! I don't want people thinking I'd abandon a puppy!

"We just have to show kids that it's spin, not fact — it's Hudson's _false_ interpretation of what happened, not what really happened," I said.

"But _how_ do we do that?" Carly asked. "Once a rumor is started, it's almost impossible to stop. It takes on a life of its own."

Carly was right. We needed a whole new campaign — right away! I stayed up late that night and made a whole new series of posters, not to get Carly elected, but to clear her name.

I think they turned out pretty good. I just hope ~~they~~ do the job!

↓

Cigarette companies used to say that smoking was GOOD for you.

Now they admit that it's hazardous to your health.

☠

How do you know what to believe?

GET THE WHOLE TRUTH!
CARLY IS
INNOCENT!!

If it looks like a duck and quacks like a duck, is it always a duck?

Yes, UNLESS it's a rubber ducky!

GET THE WHOLE TRUTH!

CARLY IS
INNOCENT!

IS THIS A PICTURE OF A CUP OR TWO PROFILES?

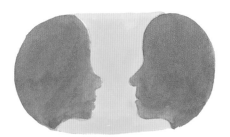

IT DEPENDS **HOW** YOU LOOK AT IT! LOOK AGAIN!

GET THE WHOLE TRUTH!
LOOK AT THE STORY FROM ANOTHER ANGLE!
CARLY IS INNOCENT!

He said she was a KEY player.

What he didn't say was that she's a DONkey...

 HEE HAW

... or a MONkey...
EEE EEE

... or a TURkey.
GOBBLE GOBBLE

GET THE <u>WHOLE</u> STORY!

CARLY IS INNOCENT!

If I told you someone had a crush on you 🩶🩶🩶   🩶🩶🩶

BUT I didn't say it was last year, 🚫🚫🚫 NOT NOW, 🚫🚫🚫

Would I be lying or telling the truth?
GET THE <u>WHOLE</u> STORY!
     CARLY IS INNOCENT!

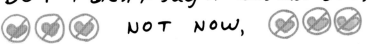

I don't know if it's enough, but it's something. Not everyone avoids Carly now, and some kids are looking at Hudson suspiciously.

Carly was looking differently at Hudson too. She was furious and couldn't wait to confront him.

How could you spread those lies about me? You knew I wouldn't abandon Munchkin. I told you I was coming back for her if no one took her.

Hey, don't get mad at me. I never said you did. All I said was the truth — you were taking this cute puppy to the animal shelter when I ran into you and offered to give the dog a home. That's the truth!

It's HALF the truth and you know it! You call that being honest? It's the same as lying! You're a total creep!

And now you're calling me names? Really, you should be thanking me for saving Munchkin's life. Everyone else is!

I would, except I'm not sure she's better off with you than at the shelter, where a nice, decent, HONEST person could have adopted her.

"He's not the least bit sorry!" Carly was so angry, she was shaking. "And the worst part is, he's getting away with it. Your posters are great and they're helping people figure out the whole truth, but not soon enough. I can't bear the thought that he'll win the election because of such an ugly smear campaign."

"Come on." I put my arm around her. "He hasn't won yet. Tomorrow's the election – we'll see what happens." I tried to sound positive, but I was worried myself.

In Study Hall I could barely focus on what Mr. L. was saying (he always welcomes us with some news tidbit). Then I heard something that caught my attention – something about the election.

Unfortunately recent elections have been more about image than substance, more about sound bites than sound policy. Before you vote tomorrow, ask yourself what you know about each candidate.

Think about how they behaved during the campaign. Don't turn your ballot into a popularity contest.

Normally I think Mr. L. is an awful person, but for today he was my favorite teacher. I hoped everyone would listen to him.

ELECTION DAY!

I was glad Carly and I had French together last period. That's when the election results were going to be announced. For most kids it was a normal school day except they took the time to vote. For Carly, Leah, and me it was the most jittery day ever. All I could think of was what would happen if we won — and what would happen if we lost. It was like being on a seesaw all day.

"Attention, students," the P.A. crackled. "The results of the Student Council election have now been tallied. For the office of treasurer — Leah Cox."

"Leah!" Carly and I jumped up from our desks and hugged each other. Leah won! And if she had won, that meant...

"...of secretary — Amelia..."

"I WON!" I screamed. I hadn't thought about ME winning, I'd been so focused on Carly. All the kids started clapping. Even Mr. Le Poivre joined in.

I hugged Carly again. "That means you won too!" I said. She grinned. We were both so relieved.

"...office of president..."

We waited for her name, ready to cheer again.

"... Hudson Strauss. Congratulations to the new Student Council, and thank you to all the candidates."

Hudson?! Not Carly? I couldn't believe it. I thought for sure that if Leah and I were elected, Carly was too. Was it some kind of mistake? Should we ask for a recount?

The worst part is that creep gets rewarded for lying.

No, I take that back— the worst part is that now he's our president. UGH! It makes me want to change schools.

I didn't know what to think. Now Leah and I would be on the Student Council WITH HUDSON! I didn't even want to be on the Student Council, not without Carly. It wasn't supposed to happen this way.

What a disaster! We have to work with that slimeball? It'll be torture!

I only ran for secretary to be with you, Carly. Maybe I should quit. Can I quit?

"No way! You can't quit!" Carly argued. "You and Leah have to balance whatever Hudson does. You need to be there now more than ever."

It wasn't what I'd imagined when we started the campaign, but I was stuck with it.

Leah → felt the same way I did — it wasn't right for us to be elected and not Carly.

Carly tried to be a good sport and told us we'd be great.

But it all felt wrong, very wrong. ←

The next day I bumped into Hudson. I thought he would be gloating, really pleased with himself for winning, but he wasn't. In fact, he almost looked scared.

"What's up?" I asked him. "Now that you're president, you're worried you might actually have to do some work?"

"Huh? No, that's not it." He practically ran away.

I wondered what was wrong, he was acting so odd. I didn't have to wait long to find out. As I sat down in Study Hall, the P.A. system came on.

"It has come to our attention that one of the candidates in yesterday's election broke the rule about respecting opponents' campaign posters. Because he took down Carly Tremain's posters, Hudson Strauss is disqualified.

The office of president goes to the candidate with the next-highest vote total, Carly Tremain."

I was stunned. Hudson _was_ the one taking down our posters! And now Carly was president? I couldn't believe it — the creep didn't get caught for his lie, but for something else! It was enough to give me back my faith in elections.

I didn't realize that Mr. L. was talking until he said something that grabbed my attention — it was about the election again.

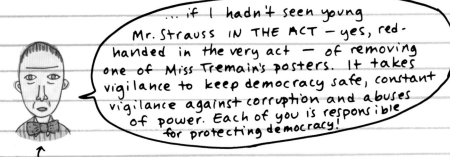

... if I hadn't seen young Mr. Strauss IN THE ACT — yes, red-handed in the very act — of removing one of Miss Tremain's posters. It takes vigilance to keep democracy safe, constant vigilance against corruption and abuses of power. Each of you is responsible for protecting democracy!

So it was Mr. L. who caught Hudson! Now he is definitely my favorite teacher, no matter how mean he acts! I'll never call him Smell-O again!

I couldn't wait to see Carly and Leah! Now we'll all be on the Student Council together, just the way we planned. And Hudson got exactly what he deserved — NOTHING! It was hard to say which was more satisfying.

There was a throng of kids around Carly after school, all congratulating her. She looked really happy.

"Great campaign!" Maya said. "I'm so glad you're president. I want to lobby you for something, for one small favor."

"Sure," said Carly. "It's my job to listen. What is it?"

"How about a candy machine, just one – in the cafeteria, not in any hallways? Please! I'm addicted to those Mellow Bars, really!" Maya pleaded.

Carly laughed. "I'll bring it up with my fellow council members, okay? I'm not promising anything more than that."

"Fine, fine," Maya said quickly. "That's great. Maybe you can make a story about it for the student news channel – 'Candy comes to school to add sweetness to classes.' Something like that."

We'd better get busy with the student TV idea. After all, the next election is only a year away.

I could see → it now.

This is Amelia with a late-breaking story about the electi It has drama, comedy a dash of mystery – who took the poster all wrapped up in a patriotic campaign But first a word from our sponsor– Mellow Bars!